For my father with tears and my son with kisses.

Cézanne and the Apple Boy • Copyright © Frances Lincoln Limited 2009

Text and illustrations copyright © Laurence Anholt 2009

The right of Laurence Anholt to be identified as the Author and Illustrator of this work has been

asserted by him in accordance with the Copyright, Designs and Patents Act, 1988

First published in Great Britain in 2009 by Frances Lincoln Limited, 4 Torriano Mews, Torriano Avenue, London NW5 2RZ

British Library Cataloguing in Publication Data available on request • ISBN 978-1-84507-910-9

Set in Impressum • Printed in China

1 3 5 7 9 8 6 4 2

PHOTOGRAPHIC CREDITS

Please note: the pages in this book are not numbered. The story begins on page 6.

Paintings by Paul Cézanne (1839–1906)

Front cover (detail): *La Montagne Sainte-Victoire above the Route du Tholonet*, 1896–8, The State Hermitage Museum, St Petersburg. Photo akg-images

Page 7: *Self-portrait*, c.1873–6, Musée d'Orsay, Paris. Photo © RMN/Hervé Lewandowski

Page 17 (above): *Hillside in Provence*, c.1890–2, The National Gallery, London. Photo © The National Gallery, London

Page 17 (below left): *House in Provence*, 1886–90, Indianapolis Museum of Art (Gift of Mrs James W. Fesler in memory of Daniel W. and Elizabeth C. Marmon)

Page 17 (below right): *Fruit and Tapestry*, c.1895–8 © The Barnes Foundation, Merion, Pennsylvania/The Bridgeman Art Library

Page 18: *Portrait of the artist's son*, c.1881–2, Musée de l'Orangerie, Paris (collection Jean Walter and Paul Guillaume). Photo © RMN/Hervé Lewandowski

Photograph of Paul Cézanne

Page 31: *Paul Cézanne with walking stick and backpack, Auvers*, c.1874 or c.1877. John Rewald Papers, National Gallery of Art, Washington, D.C., Gallery Archives

Cézanne
and the Apple Boy

LAURENCE ANHOLT

FRANCES LINCOLN

PAUL was playing with his friends
when his mother brought a letter,

"Look!" she said. "It's from your father!"

Paul had not seen his father for a long time.
He knew that he was an artist who lived far away in
the countryside. And Paul had exactly the same name
as his father. It was written on all of his school books:

Paul read the letter...

Dear Paul,
I would like you to visit me.
The countryside is
beautiful.
I think you are old
enough to come on a
Painting Expedition
in the mountains.
With love from
your father,
Paul Cézanne

Then something fell out of the envelope.

It was a train ticket.

His mother packed some food in a little bag.
She put him on the train and kissed him goodbye.

It was a long journey and the
jogging of the train put Paul to sleep.

When he woke up, he saw a mountain.

Paul walked out of the station and
into the little town. At last he found
his father's house, but there was
no one at home.

"I'll tell you where you'll find him,"
said a lady. "Half way up the
mountain, painting crazy pictures!"

So Paul stepped onto the
winding path which led out
of the town and into the
mountains. It was very hot
and the path was steep.

In the shade of a tree, a donkey was munching apples.

Someone was talking to himself nearby.

Paul peeped round the corner.

"OH!" he shouted.

High on a rocky path
was a man as big as a bear.
He was making a wild
painting. He had a wild
beard and wild eyes.

Paul ran back down the path.

"Paul, Paul! Don't you remember?
I am Paul Cézanne – the same as you!
I am your father."

Cézanne was as big as the mountain
but he spoke gently.
"I am very pleased to see you," he said.
"But I will not shake your hand...
You see, I do not like anyone touching me."

Then the mountain man packed up his paints,
and set off along the path.

"We are going on a journey right to the top of
the blue mountain," said Cézanne. "It's a long way,
but if we follow the path, we won't get lost.

"We haven't got much money,
but look, we have plenty of apples...
and plenty of paints and canvasses.

"You look after the donkey.
And I'll look after you."

When it grew dark,
they made a fire by a little stream.

"Tomorrow I will make a picture of you,"
said Cézanne. "But you will have to sit
as still as an apple."

Then they fell asleep
under the stars.

When Paul woke up, Cézanne was sorting his paintings.

"You see, Paul," he said, "I am inventing a new kind of painting...

"I make everything into simple shapes. I paint houses like boxes, and trees like cones. Everything has a shape."

"What shape am I?" said Paul.

"You are as round as a sweet little apple!"

They followed the winding path through
a valley and into a dusty village.

The people in the café stared at Cézanne and laughed at his pictures.

"What have you painted today?" they snorted. "A wonky house or a wobbly tree!"

"You see, Paul," his father sighed, "the world doesn't understand me and I don't understand the world. That's why I spend my time on the mountains..."

"...And that's why you are so poor, Mountain Man!" laughed the people in the café. Cézanne stood up and walked towards the door.

"Just a moment," said a voice behind them. "May I see that picture?"

Paul turned round.

A man with a bow tie and an expensive
suit was staring at his painting.

"This is extraordinary,"
he said. "I would like to
take this picture back to
my art gallery in the city.

"My name is Vollard.
I am a picture dealer and
I am always looking for
exciting new work..."

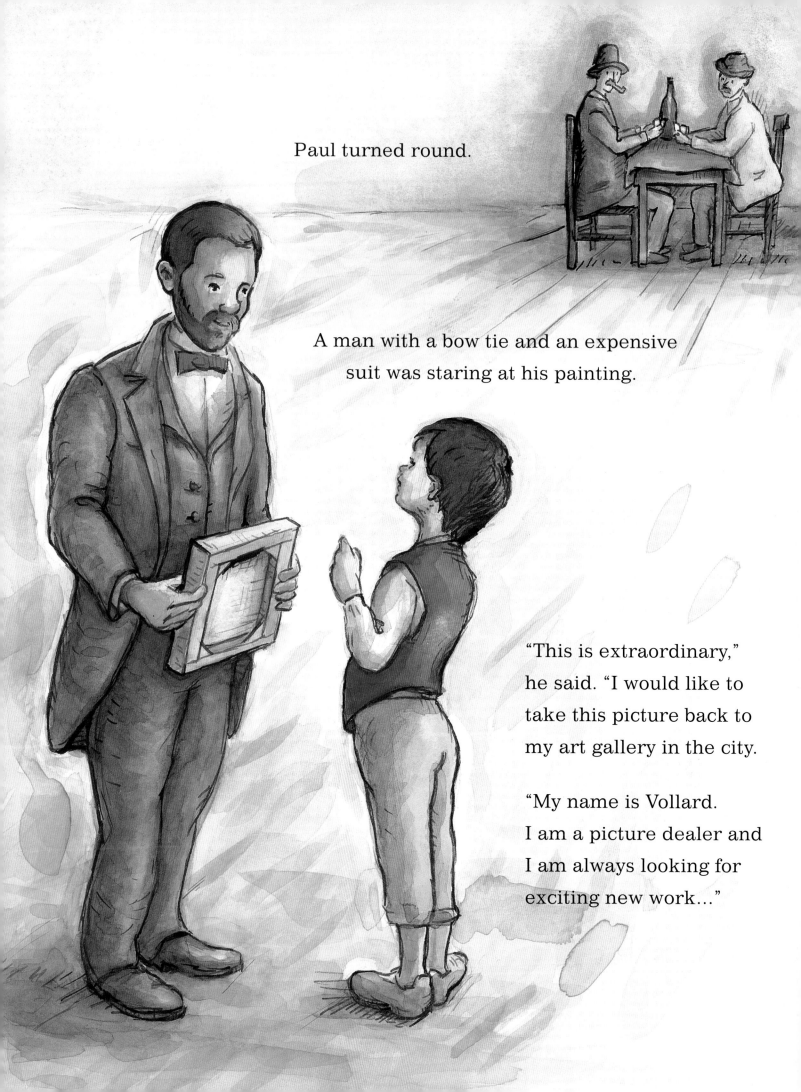

"Well, we have more paintings than we can carry," said Cézanne.
"Take as many as you like... Have this one ... and this one!"

So Vollard left with a huge pile of pictures.

Paul ran after him. "Please, Mr Vollard,"
he whispered. "Look after these paintings.
I think they are very special. I think
my father has invented a new kind
of painting."

Then Paul helped his father pack up his paints.
As they walked out of the dusty village,
they could hear the people laughing.

"Ah, Paul," said Cézanne, "sometimes
life is as hard as climbing a mountain."

"The people are right,
my paintings are
worth nothing at all."

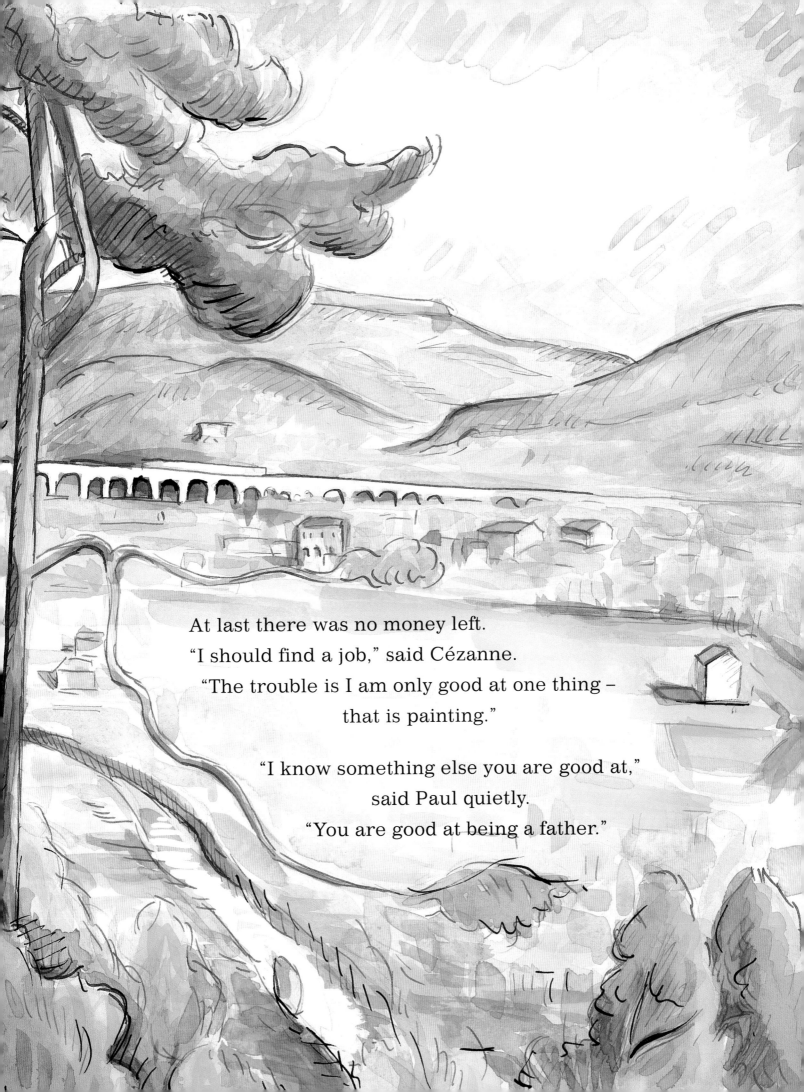

At last there was no money left.
"I should find a job," said Cézanne.
"The trouble is I am only good at one thing –
that is painting."

"I know something else you are good at,"
said Paul quietly.
"You are good at being a father."

Far away Paul saw a tiny man, waving his arms and shouting.
When he came closer, Paul could see the man was dressed
in an expensive suit with a bow tie – It was Vollard!

"Quick, Paul," he panted, "where is your father?"

"My father is working," said Paul. "If you want to buy a picture,
you will have to talk to me."

Vollard laughed. "Listen," he said,
"the whole of Paris is talking about
the Mountain Man. They say he has
invented a new kind of painting."

"Of course," said Paul.
"My father is the
greatest painter
in the world."

"What's all this noise?" said Cézanne, coming round the corner.

"I'm trying to explain," said Vollard, "I have sold every one of your paintings! All this money is for you! I want to buy more – as many as you can paint!"

Cézanne stuffed the money in his pocket.

"Thank you very much, Mr Vollard. I would like to shake you by the hand … but you see, I don't like anybody touching me.

"Now if you will excuse me; Paul and I have to leave. We are nearly at the top of our mountain."

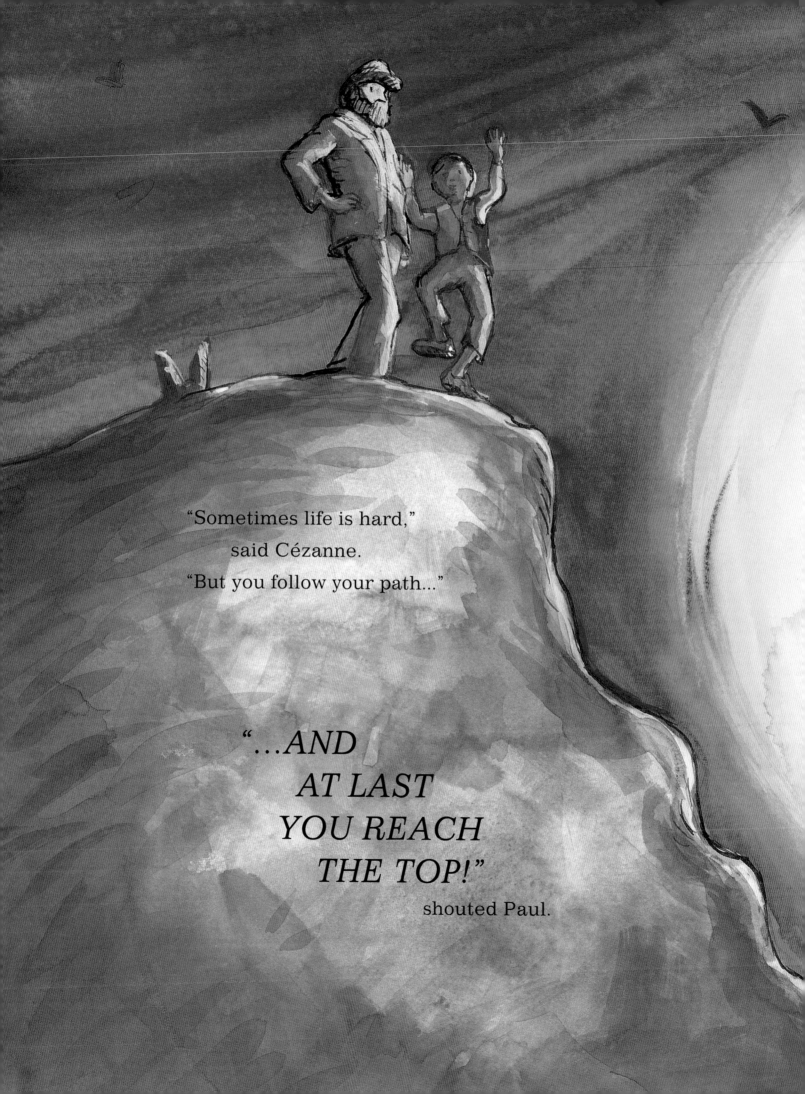

"Sometimes life is hard,"
said Cézanne.
"But you follow your path..."

"...AND
AT LAST
YOU REACH
THE TOP!"
shouted Paul.

Then Paul and his father walked
back down the mountain. When
they reached the dusty village,
Paul was afraid that the people would
laugh. But he pulled himelf up tall.

"I am the son of the Mountain Man,"
he whispered.

The summer was ending
and the apple trees were
golden-brown. At last
they reached the little town.
And there was Cézanne's
house near the station.

Paul ran so fast he almost
knocked over his mother
who was waiting to take him home.

"Oh Paul!" she said, "I hardly recognised you. You have grown so tall."

"Well, Paul," said his father, "we had a good expedition. I would like
to shake you by the hand, but…

but…"

"…But I will give you
a big kiss instead!"
said Paul.

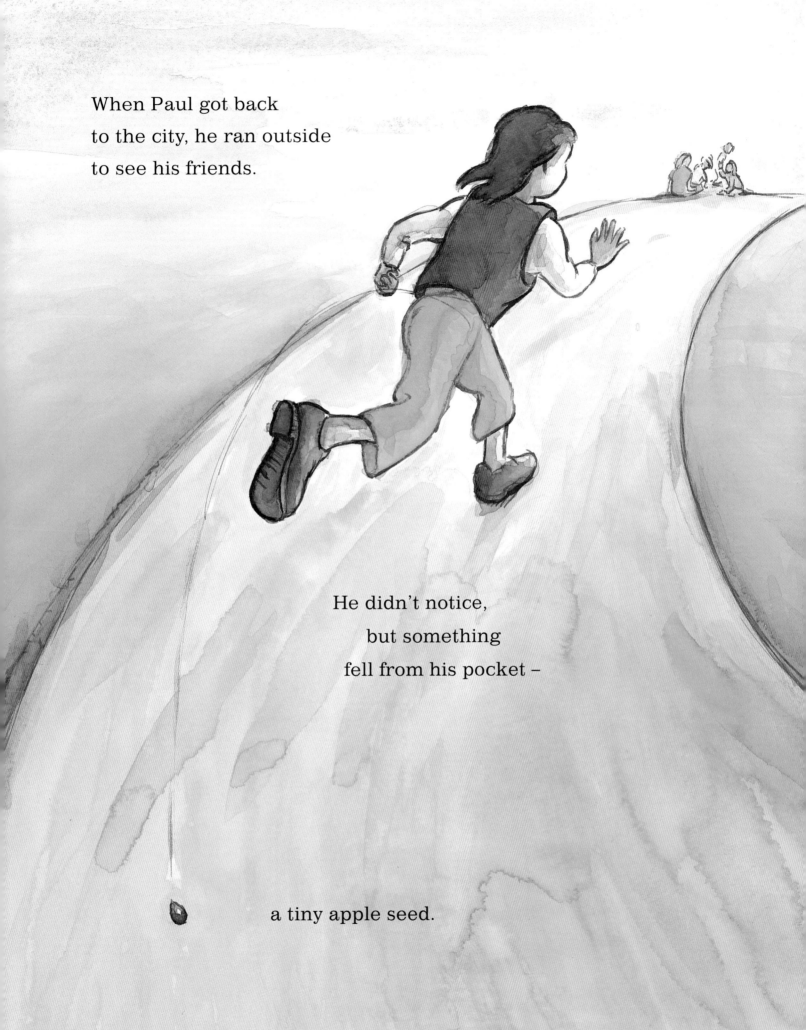

When Paul got back
to the city, he ran outside
to see his friends.

He didn't notice,
but something
fell from his pocket –

a tiny apple seed.

Ten years passed by. Paul looked outside where the tiny seed had grown into an apple tree which blossomed in the spring. He thought of his father, Paul Cézanne, following his path, high on the blue mountain.

He had became a successful picture dealer like Vollard. He sold his father's paintings all over the world where people paid millions for the mountains, the wonky houses and the piles of apples on wobbly tables.